Book Publishers Network
P. O. Box 2256
Bothell, WA 98041
425-483-3040
www.bookpublishersnetwork.com

10 9 8 7 6 5 4 3 2 1

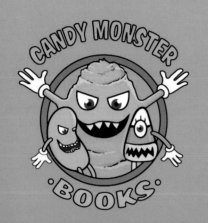

Printed in the United States of America

LCCN: 2018951131
ISBN: 978-1-948963-07-7

@FrankMusta
You Tube The Adventures of Frank and Mustar
The Adventures of Frank and Mustar
FrankandMustard.com

Special Dedication

To Aaron Miles, Jennifer Korns, Joshua Hoover, Teresa Vail, Shawn Landry, Jessica Batson, Mike Cummings, Arturo Alvarez, Jamie Lynn, and Heath Scatton. Thank you for taking me out to experience the thrill of catching my first wave! Yes, it was a little scary, but I will never forget the exhilarating feeling of riding that wave all the way to shore. Thank you to everyone who helped me make it happen. I truly appreciate being included.

R.I.P. Rugger - You were an amazing dog!

Executive Producers

The Doleman Family

Editorial Credits

Kristina Oldani

Producer Credits

Julie Godden, BritBratThisAndThat, Nancy, Charlie, & Greyson Butros, Giana Portugal, Cindy and Vic's R&R, Inc., Vicki Hall, Adam & Meredith Wessling, Ryan Casey, Jakobe, Mieke, Arjen, Chris and Michaela Doleman, The Sullivan-Wilkison family, Kyle Hackney, The Cooper Family, The Davidson Family, Neil and Becky Manning

Supporter Credits

Leah Fenner, Treasure Chest, Liz and Kelly Brown, A Child's Dream Preschool, Tommy Weaver, Cindy and Vic's R&R, Inc., Mila and Drake Fernandez, Bryce, Rachel, & Emberlei Paulson, Milo & Otto Murphy, Mrs. Amsden, Vicki Hall, Adam & Meredith Wessling, Bella Rose Martineau and Jackie Johnson, Wyatt and David Dunlap, The Burdak Family, Steve and Annie Butros, Patrick Harkins and Kasey Manning, Ryan Casey, Robert, Sherry & Erik Meyers, Jakobe, Mieke and Arjen Doleman, Mary Holmberg, Chris and Michaela Doelman, The Canaan Family, BritBratThisAndThat, The Buendels, Kristin Martinez, Riffer, The Sullivan-Wilkison family, Connie Fenner, Kyle Hackney, Moshe Stanislowski, Laurel & Linnea Jozkowski, The Cooper Family, Jordan Deja and Korina Zamora-Deja, Opal Schell, Esker Peters, Kalli & Penny Davidson, Julie Godden

1

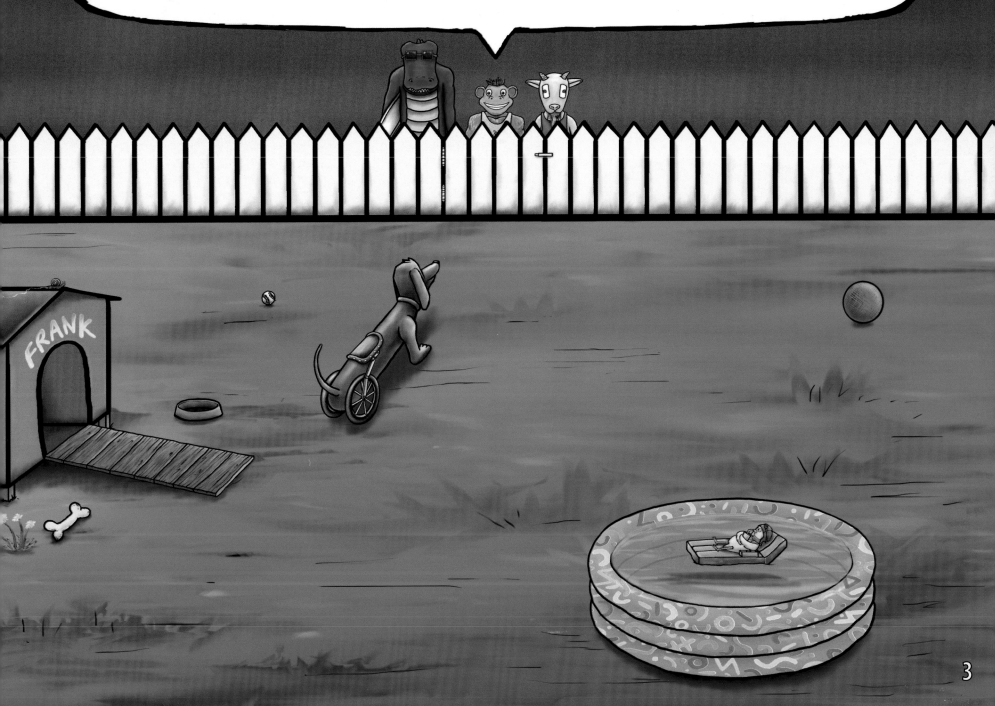

Hey, our friends are over there!

15

21

22

23

27

31

34

35

39

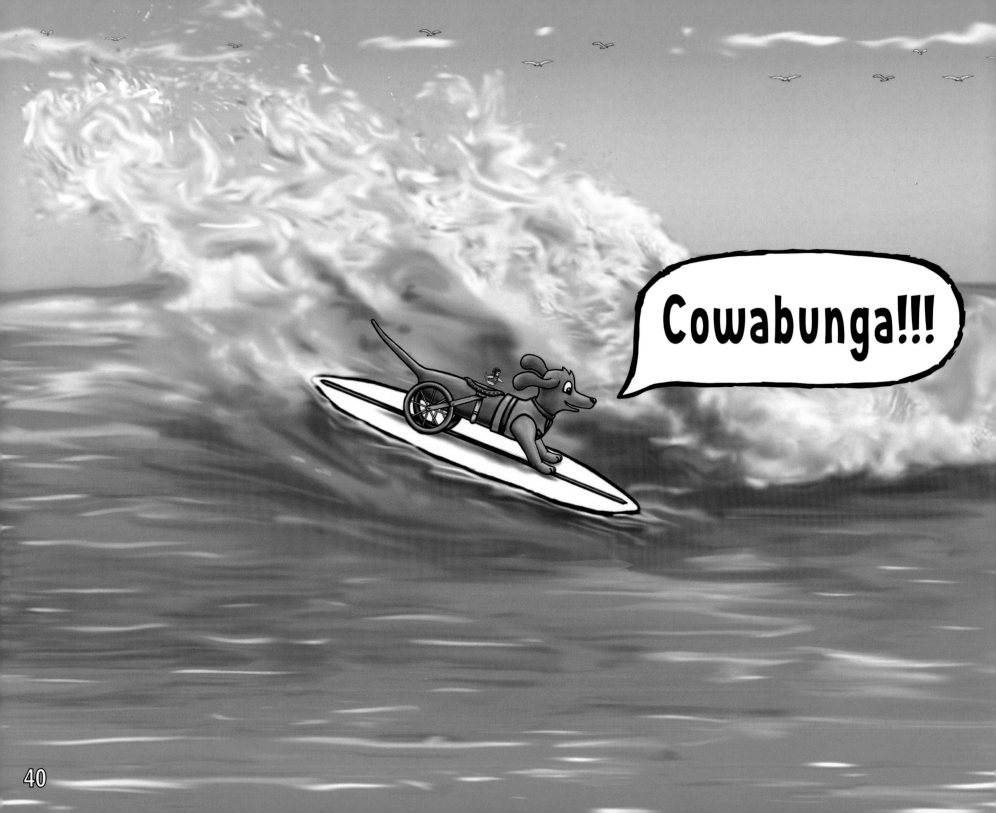

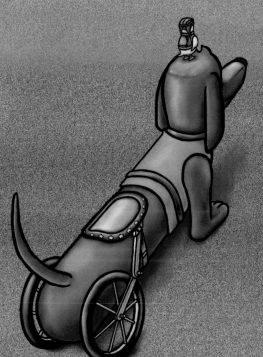

Thanks for including us, Miles! We couldn't have done it without everyone's support!

45

THE END

1. What did you enjoy most about reading this book?

2. Who is your favorite character? Why?

3. How do you think Frank felt when Miles invited him to go surfing?

4. What does inclusion mean?

5. How can we make sure that we include people with differences?

6. Do you think that it took courage for Frank to go surfing? Why or why not?

7. Do you have the courage to try something new?

8. Can you strike a pose?

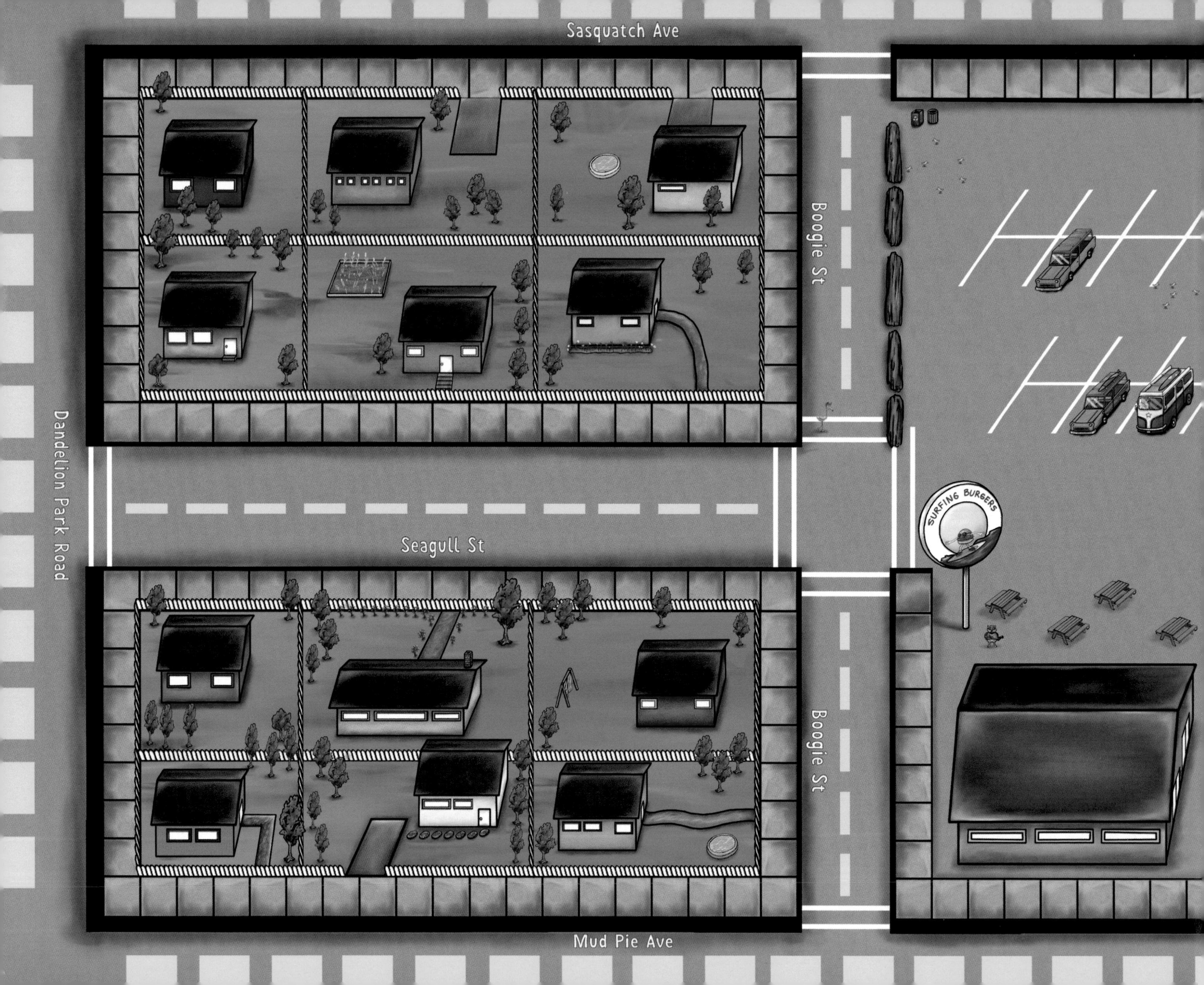

Sasquatch Ave

Boogie St

SURFING BURGERS

Dandelion Park Road

Seagull St

Boogie St

Mud Pie Ave

Mud Pie Ave

WHEELS AND WAVES

ASSEMBLY INFORMATION

Awesome

Motivational

Compelling

Inspirational

Perseverance

Engaging

Teamwork

Courageous

Growth Mindset

Positive Attitude

Leadership Skills

Disability Awareness

Adventurous

Educational

After suffering a life changing injury in 2002, Simon Calcavecchia traveled down many different paths until he discovered a life of passion. After overcoming numerous obstacles while dealing with quadriplegia, he discovered his purpose in life by becoming a children's book author and a motivational speaker.

Simon's assembly presentation covers a spectrum of topics such as living with quadriplegia, having a growth mindset, a sense of adventure and persevering through life's challenges. He demonstrates these qualities through videos, music and his compelling story. If you would like Simon to come to your school, then please visit www.FrankandMustard.com.

"It was one of the best assemblies I have ever seen! I have been in education over 25 years, so that says a lot! You are changing lives, Simon... truly changing lives!"
- Principal at Grand Mound Elementary

"Simon was fabulous. He was engaging and inspiring. I would highly recommend him for any assembly!"
- Principal at Boston Harbor Elementary

"Simon was honest, kind, and inspirational. Our students listened and watched in awe as he told his story."
-Teacher at Serendipity Academy

"I think that Simon's message will have a really big impact on the culture of our school and how our students think about disabilities in the future."
-Principal at Marshall Middle School

ABOUT THE ARTiST

Arturo Alvarez was born with a passion to create and has dedicated his life to developing his artistic skills. He studied the Fine Arts at Long Beach Community College, in California. After that, he formed a screen printing business that combined his drawing and graphic design skills. For nine years, Arturo operated a successful screen printing business. The success came from an active approach to collaboration, attendance to community events and assistance to aspiring artists and entrepreneurs.

In 2014, Arturo moved to Washington where he met Simon Calcavecchia. At the time, Simon was leading the construction of a giant Komodo Dragon float that mounted onto his wheelchair for the Procession of the Species. The procession is a parade that takes place in Olympia, Washington every spring. While working on the project together, they became really good friends. They also continued to collaborate on many projects and eventually created The Adventures of Frank and Mustard. This children's book series has created many opportunities for both Arturo and Simon to inspire, educate, and motivate youth throughout the Pacific Northwest.

You can contact Arturo at alvarezarturo31@yahoo.com. To see more of his work check out his Instagram page @your_pencil